The Gigantic Baby

BY **MORDICAI GERSTEIN** • ILLUSTRATED BY **ARNIE LEVIN**

HarperCollins*Publishers*

The Gigantic Baby
Text copyright © 1991 by Mordicai Gerstein
Illustrations copyright © 1991 by Arnold Levin
Printed in the U.S.A. All rights reserved.
1 2 3 4 5 6 7 8 9 10
First Edition

Library of Congress Cataloging-in-Publication Data

Gerstein, Mordicai.
   The gigantic baby / by Mordicai Gerstein ; illustrated by Arnie
Levin.
       p.   cm.
   Summary: The more a baby cries, the more she grows, until her
brother thinks of a way to reverse the process and turn his gigantic
sister into a normal-sized infant.
   ISBN 0-06-022074-0. — ISBN 0-06-022106-2 (lib. bdg.)
   [1. Babies—Fiction.   2. Brothers and sisters—Fiction.   3. Size—
Fiction.]   I. Levin, Arnie, ill.   II. Title
PZ7.G325Gi 1991   90-35537
[E]—dc20   CIP
                                                                AC

The illustrations in this book were done in pen and ink, watercolors, and pastels.

For Risa, who has a wonderful laugh
and for Harry Hess, whose laugh was unforgettable
—M.G.

For Pamela
—A.L.

An icy drizzle was falling the morning that Marvin's parents brought home the baby. It was wrapped in armfuls of pink flannel and had a tiny pink puckered face.

"Meet your sister," they said, but she didn't look like a sister. She was bald and just looked like a baby.

"She's so tiny," said Marvin.

"Don't worry," said his mother, "babies grow fast."

She slept all day that first day, and everyone whispered. On the second day she woke up and started to cry. It was a small cry. Marvin's mother picked up the baby and fed her. The crying stopped. Later it started again. The baby cried till Marvin went to bed. The crying woke him in the middle of the night. It went on and on. The full moon out the window looked like a crying baby's face. Marvin finally fell asleep again.

In the morning the baby was still crying. When Marvin got to school, everyone asked about his new baby sister.

"She seems to cry a lot," he told them.

After school the baby was still crying. Marvin's father carried her around and around the living room. He sang "Rock-a-bye, Baby." He sang "Hush, Little Baby, Don't You Cry."

The baby kept crying. He sang Navajo rain dances.

He sang grand opera. Nothing helped.

The baby cried all through the third night and woke Marvin twice. Her crying filled the house. It got louder and louder. In the morning, after Marvin's mother fed her, the baby cried some more.

"The poor thing," said his mother, looking weary. "I don't know why she cries so much, but just look how she's grown." The baby had burst out of her little gown, and had completely outgrown her bunting. Marvin remembered how lost she had looked in them when they first brought her home. Her crying was louder, too.

The doctor came to examine her.

"There's nothing wrong with this baby," said the doctor. "It's just the colic that makes her cry, and no one knows what colic is. But I've never seen a baby grow like this. She's twice as big as when she was born!"

Every day the baby cried, and every day she grew bigger. The louder she cried, the more she grew. The more she grew, the more she ate. The more she ate, the louder she cried; and the louder she cried, the more she grew. She outgrew her basket and cried in her crib. After a week the crib bulged and sagged with the baby's weight. It took Marvin's mother and father both to lift her out of it. Staggering and groaning, they carried the huge screaming infant into Marvin's room.

"We hope you don't mind sleeping on the couch for a while, dear," his mother shouted over the screams. "We need your bed for the baby till we get a crib big enough."

"Where will you get a crib that big?" said Marvin, but his parents couldn't hear him.

Soon, only the living room was big enough for the baby. Marvin's parents covered the floor with mattresses, and used the carpets for diapers. A tank truck full of milk parked in front of the house, and a hose came in through the window with a huge nipple that went right into the baby's mouth.

Marvin's sister was now big enough to pick him up in one hand. He was afraid she might grab him and put him in her mouth, so he would tiptoe into the room, carefully climb up on her shoulder, and then sing right in her ear.

He sang "Old MacDonald Had a Farm."

He sang "The Star-Spangled Banner."

He shouted the story of Goldilocks and the three bears, changing his
voice for each part. Nothing helped. She howled and yowled louder.

The baby's screams filled the street, and at night they kept the whole neighborhood awake. One day her shrieks broke windows blocks away at Marvin's school. The teachers had to shout to be heard.

One afternoon Marvin came home and found a big trailer truck and a crane parked in front of his house. There were TV cameras and police cars, and people watching. The baby had grown too big for the house. The crane took the roof off and then lifted the howling infant onto the truck. They drove her to an old airplane hangar way out of town. It was the only place big enough to hold her, and far enough away so most people couldn't hear her.

A fleet of milk trucks lined up to feed her. Her diapers were old circus tents, and she had to be changed by big construction cranes and tractors. Firefighters washed her with fire hoses.

Teams of doctors came to examine her. They listened to her heart with seismographs made to measure earthquakes. They looked into her ears with telescopes. They looked down her throat using big sheets of plywood to hold down her tongue.

"This baby is perfectly normal," they all said. "It's just the colic that makes her cry, and no one knows what colic is."

"What we do know," said one of the doctors, "is that the more she cries, the bigger she gets. At her present growth rate, she'll cover the nation in three more weeks. In six weeks, she'll outgrow the earth." They discussed sending her to another, larger planet.

As Marvin listened to the doctors, he got an idea. It seemed so simple he was sure it must be silly, but he took a chance and spoke up.

"Why don't you try to get her to laugh?" he said. "If she laughs she can't cry, and she'll stop growing."

The doctors and his parents looked at each other. By now the baby had outgrown the hangar. She had kicked the roof off and screamed straight up at the cloudy night sky.

"It's worth a try," said his father.

"Yes," said the others. "It might help, and it can't hurt."

At first they tried tickling her feet with the leaves of palm trees. That only made her cry more.

Then they painted clown faces on blimps and balloons that sailed back and forth in front of her.

They hung enormous teddy bears and rattles from helicopters hovering overhead.

But she cried louder and harder, and blew them all out to sea.

She cried so hard and loud, she blew all the clouds away, and suddenly, right in front of the baby, there was the full moon, like a fat grinning face, glowing with silvery light. The baby looked up and stopped crying. People miles away who'd gotten used to her wailing were wakened by the silence.

The baby looked at the moon for the first time. She reached out a hand toward it and smiled. Then she giggled. It sounded like hundreds of glass wind chimes. Then she laughed, and it sounded to Marvin like mountain springs when the snow melts after a long winter. Great fluffy clouds sailed by and covered and uncovered the moon.

"Look!" cried Marvin. "They're playing peek-a-boo with her!" The baby laughed and laughed.

She giggled and cooed.

And then she fell asleep.

Marvin and his parents and all the doctors looked up at the sleeping baby. She looked much smaller. They all cheered, very, very quietly, so as not to wake her.

After that, she hardly cried at all, and in only a few weeks, she was a normal-sized baby sleeping in her crib at home. Marvin looked in at her and saw she was awake. He covered his face and said, "Peek-a-boo!" as he uncovered it. The baby laughed so happily that Marvin laughed too.

"You're really a very nice little sister," said Marvin. Her name was Risa, which means "laughter."

"Someday," Marvin said to her, "I'll tell you all about how you cried and cried and grew to be gigantic." Risa looked at him and giggled. "Don't you believe me?" he asked her. She laughed and crowed.

"You know," said Marvin, "I can hardly believe it myself!"

Then they were both laughing.